The Deportee

Kyuka Lilymjok

ISBN 978-978-962-004-3

Published by:
Free Pen Publishers
10 Lachlan Close Maitama, Abuja

Any people depicted in stock imagery provided by Thinkstock are models, and such images are being used for such purposes only.

This book is printed on acid-free paper.

The views expressed in this work are solely those of the author and do not necessarily reflect the views of the publisher. The publisher hereby disclaims any responsibility for them.

To my wife Maria and my children: Justice, Sunfair and Fairprincess

There is no having
the broken pot; neither
is there having
its water

Chapter One

Coming down from the plane that brought him from Russia, Morgan took a cursory look at the Murtala Mohammed International Airport he flew to Russia from thirty years ago. Nothing much has changed in the airport. It was still very much the airport he knew thirty years ago – a far cry from Vnukovo international airport Moscow.

Standing alone under the scorching Lagos sun, Morgan was yet to come to terms with the fact that he had been deported from Russia. He had in his right hand a briefcase which was as brief as his body frame and indeed the clothes he wore. Tall, light complexioned with slightly broad shoulders that matched his frame, he appeared undecided about something as he began walking towards a cluster of taxis in the airport he had landed an hour ago.

As he moved towards the column of taxis, a bevy of taxi drivers who hitherto had been looking at him with a certain measure of disinterest surged forward towards him all clamoring to have him as a passenger. '*Ogar, come enter my motor, it get air condition and e dey cheap well well; ogar I go give you good fare and you go like the way I go drive; ogar no mind them, na me go carry you go where you dey go and I go collect anything you give me,*' the taxi drivers besieged him from every direction.

He ignored all their offers and walked past them further down the road. When he first came out of the airport building, they had rushed at him, but he had hushed their rush with his hand which told them he was not in a haste to leave the airport. Now he had brushed aside their second rush by walking past them to look for a taxi outside the airport. He had been told how exorbitant their fares were and he needed every nickel he had. Outside the airport, he had been told he could get a taxi for half the fare he would pay for one inside the airport.

Outside the airport, two taxis drove by. The one in front looked like it was carrying all the dust and fatigue of Lagos on its body and its engine sounded like it was being strangled by a garrote wire.

The second taxi looked like it had no soul and if it had, must have either forgotten its soul at home when driven out by the driver or lost it on the way. The driver inside the taxi looked no better than his vehicle. He looked soulless and lost to both heaven and hell.

The third taxi was an improvement over the first two. Morgan flagged it down. It screeched to a halt beside him. 'Victoria Island,' he said.

'Where in Victoria Island?' the taxi driver asked. Dark and stout, the taxi driver had the face of a bulldog chewing wasps. It was the kind of face only a mother could love.

Taking his eyes from the face of the taxi driver, Morgan consulted a piece of paper in his hand. '27 Ahmadu Bello Way,' he said.

For a while, the taxi driver did not say anything. From the way his face was working, he was consulting his memory and trying to determine how much to charge. It did not take him long to do both. 'Four thousand naira,' he said.

Outside the airport and four thousand naira? Jeez! Morgan thought. 'Two thousand naira,' he said.

'Three thousand naira,' the taxi driver said, beginning to pull away.

Morgan thinking he was bluffing watched him pull away believing he would stop moving and reverse to him, but he did not. Shrugging his shoulders, he waited for the next taxi which did not take long coming.

The driver of the fourth taxi reminded him of a rascal he knew before he went to Russia. The Governor of a state wanted to employ rascals as Traffic Regulations Enforcement Corps. The rascal young men and women of the state turned up for the interview including the rascal he knew. When the Governor walked into the interview venue for the interview, the rascal he knew standing alone and smoking weeds in a corner of the venue, walked to the Governor and blew smoke into the Governor's face. There and then the Governor declared him head of the Traffic Regulations Enforcement Corps. If he could blow smoke into his face, he could deal ruthlessly with any driver who violates traffic regulations. Recalling the rascal and his engagement by the Governor, Morgan also recalled what the Governor told the Traffic Regulations Enforcement Corps when inaugurating them: 'Anyone you arrest for flouting traffic regulations and he speaks English to you, his fine is five thousand naira,' the Governor told them. Knowing most of the street urchins he engaged as traffic corps could not speak English being either school dropouts or throw-outs, traffic offenders were likely to take advantage of their lack of proficiency in English by speaking the language to intimidate and scare them away from penalizing them, the Governor had stipulated this penalty as an antidote.

Morgan smiled to himself.

The taxi driver puzzled by his smile looked mildly confounded.

'Victoria Island,' Morgan said to the taxi driver.

'Where in Victoria Island?' the taxi driver asked him.

'27 Ahmadu Bello Way,' he said.

'Three thousand naira,' the taxi driver said.

'Two thousand naira.'

'Two thousand five hundred naira,' the taxi driver said beginning to drive away like the previous driver.

'OK, OK,' Morgan said, flagging him down and hurrying down the road after the taxi. When he got to it, he scrambled in and pulled the door to close it. But the seatbelt of the taxi was hanging out and the contact of the door with the metal slip of the seatbelt gave up a jarring sound that set his teeth on edge.

'The seatbelt, the seatbelt,' the taxi driver said bending across Morgan to pull the seatbelt in. Doing so brought his face closer to Morgan's face and he could perceive a faint smell he could not ascribe to any smell he knew. Unable to assign it to any distinct smell, he concluded it was the smell of liquor, sweat and dirt all mixed up.

Chapter Two

On the way, the taxi driver wound up the glasses and put on the air conditioner whose fan appeared to be in overdrive while its cooling system by all effect was off duty. The fan was spurting dust and seemed to be drawing the faint odor in the driver and ramming it into Morgan's nose.

'Please, wind down the windows and put off the air conditioner,' Morgan said when he could no longer bear the suffocating conditions in the cab.

'Ogar, the air condition will soon start cooling,' the taxi driver said with a marked unwillingness to do what Morgan had requested.

'We have covered up to two kilometres and I am yet to feel any chill from the air conditioner and you are telling me it will soon start cooling?' Morgan quipped 'Well, I can't wait for it to start cooling,' he said, pushing down the winding button on his side. But the glass by his side did not wind down. The button was faulty.

The driver seeing he was being driven to distraction and desperation quickly rolled down the glasses using the roll-down button on his side. As soon as the glasses were down, a stream of moist air poured into the car. Though it was not exactly soothing, it was a lot better than what was there before. Morgan heaved a sigh of relief.

Soon they ran into a traffic snarl-up. The snarl-up was by a T-junction. It was caused by drivers refusing to obey traffic light at the T-junction. Traffic policemen had been drafted to the scene to untangle the snarl, but were yet to do so, not for lack of effort and time to do so, but because drivers were disobeying their directives as they had disobeyed the traffic light. Now a lane meant for two vehicles was plied by four.

The snarl in the traffic was on the faces of the drivers that caused it. Inside the vehicles that thronged the road, people were snarling, cursing and swearing at each other as if snarls, curses and swearing would dissolve the jam in the traffic. Obeying the traffic policemen which would have dissolved the tangle they were unwilling to.

In his vehicle, Morgan could hear two drivers cursing and swearing at each other:

'Your father.'

'Your mother.'

'God punish you.'

'The devil is already punishing you.'

'Go to hell!'

'You are already in one!'

'What a way to welcome me home,' Morgan mused under his breath. To his taxi driver, he said, 'Is it always like this? I have been away from Naija for thirty years.'

'Lucky you,' the driver said, forlorn in voice and face. 'It may not always be like this, but is frequently like this. Indiscipline in the land fans out into corruption, greed and impatience. While greed and corruption are our blight in offices, greed and impatience is our scourge on the roads.'

'Hmm ...,' Morgan droned. The Nigeria he knew was very much alive and working the way he knew it before going to Russia.

'Traffic light was designed on the assumption it would regulate intelligent drivers with discipline to obey it,' the taxi driver went on in a bitter tone. 'This assumption does not hold true here. Here drivers driven by greed and impatience as their vehicles were driven by them, stupidly disobey traffic light by running red lights. What can traffic light do? Driven by greed, they run amok the road to *loot* it the way politicians run amok public resources to loot them. Every driver wanting to *eat* the road at the same time, there is always no road for anyone.

'Hmm ...' Morgan hummed. The more the driver spoke, the more he was becoming convinced he must be a very educated person.

As the case is with traffic light, it is with democracy. Democracy was evolved on the assumption it would be operated by moral and honorable human beings who, when they commit a moral or legal wrong, would heed the rules of the game and red-card themselves by resigning without a referee doing so; what do you see here? Elected and appointed public office holders do abominable things in office; when found out, they lack the honor and morality to resign until they are forced out. What can democracy do? Democracy was also evolved on the assumption of trust; on the assumption elected representatives of the people can be trusted to represent honestly those who elected them; what do you find here? The law as a whole evolved on the assumption it would not be flouted en masse and that judges who give effect to the law would be honorable and honest in their guardianship of the law; what do you see here? The whole assumptions on which modern society is founded do not hold true here, what can anyone do? We lack the moral software needed to operate democracy and even the law, what can democracy or the law do?'

'Hmm ...,' Morgan groaned again, squirming under the unrelenting Lagos heat. Since they ran into the hold-up, heat in the car had jumped, not through the roof, but on him. What the taxi driver, who he later hailed an elite taxi driver, was saying also did not help matters. It was increasing the heat for him. 'The heat. It is so boiling hot,' he whimpered.

'This is Lagos,' the driver said in a throaty voice. 'In Lagos, heat and mosquitoes are in an unholy alliance – heat lays people bare for mosquitoes to feast on them. I learned though there is heat in hell, there are no mosquitoes.'

Morgan laughed in spite of himself. 'Tough,' he whirred.

'Baking is the word. This is the kind of heat that made a man just arriving Nigeria from Europe to ask what the Nigerian Government was doing about the weather.'

Again, Morgan laughed against the grind of the heat. 'Everyone is frowning and cursing,' he said, sounding depressed.

'Because the economy is frowning and cursing,' the taxi driver said, pertly. 'When the economy smiles, people will smile.'

'You sound quite educated.'

'I hold a masters degree in engineering?'

'What!'

'Yes, I am a masters degree holder in engineering. But the only thing my degrees in engineering have done for me all these years is to engineer poverty for me.'

'Again, Morgan laughed against the flow of mood. 'Black man don suffer,' he said after a moment of silence. 'No good job for him in the white man's country because of racial discrimination ...'

'And no good job for him in his own country because of corruption,' the taxi driver completed for him. 'We are caught in a double bind of frustration. I have a friend who is a graduate of sociology. Like me, he has no job. As I lament my degrees in engineering have only engineered poverty for me, he laments all his degree in sociology has done for him is to socialize him with poverty.'

'If there is something we don't lack here, it is good sense of humor,' Morgan said, laughing.

'Without it, we are awaiting patients of hypertension, depression and dementia,' the taxi driver intoned.

'It is bad.'

'It is indeed bad.'

'Caught between the devil and the deep blue sea, we may laugh at both the devil and the deep blue sea.'

'That is madness.'

'You got it. Madness seems our only path to mercy and happiness.'

'Before we take to madness, we will stay entertained in this huge theatre of tragedy by our good sense of humor and comic tales that bubble around the country like popped champagne,' the taxi driver said, a faint smile on his face expanding. 'Just coming into the country, you might not have heard this funny story I am about telling you,' he went on beaming with smiles.

'Sure, I am not likely to have heard it. Please tell me. I am all ears,' Morgan said, excitedly.

'A guy toasted a girl. The girl looking contemptuously at him asked him who he was to toast her.'

"I am the GM of Gymsum Products Company Limited," the guy proudly said to her.

The girl melted with excitement. She was being courted by the General Manager of a company. She collected his office address. She went to great lengths to dress well for a visit to the guy's workplace. On getting to the office, she met the guy at the gate. "What are you doing at the gate?" she asked with a sinking heart. Shebi, you said you are the GM?"

"*Nham*," the guy retorted. 'Gate Man now."

'Breaking into tears, the girl was wondering where she would get money to repay a small loan she took to dress well for the visit.'

Morgan laughed for a long while. Laughing, he was no longer feeling the heat the way he felt it before.

After about forty minutes inside the traffic holdup, Morgan's taxi driver was able to pull through the traffic jam. On the third mainland bridge, Morgan could see makeshifts and sleazy human habitations constructed mainly with either corrugated zinc or planks of wood littering the shore of the sea. Those constructed with corrugated zinc, the zinc has been eaten by rust; had turned completely brown and must be leaking in several places. Those constructed with wood, the wood has turned black in virtually the whole settlements. These settlements were mainly in the occupation of fishermen who eked their livelihood from the sea. A few were occupied by poor people who could not afford accommodation on land. Finding they could not pay exorbitant rents demanded by landlords, they rushed to the sea shore to put up the jumbled structures that lined the shore. Not firm on the ground, these structures seemed to sway with the tidal movement of the sea. Floating on the sea by the settlements and far from them were canoes owned and used by the fishermen

On the third mainland bridge, whiff after whiff of rot from timber and canoes buried in sea water wafted through the open windows of the taxi Morgan was. Strangely, instead of him wincing in distaste, he found the smell aromatic and was sniffing it in delight.

'Caught between the devil and the deep blue sea,' Morgan repeated to himself his earlier expression as the taxi sped on the third mainland bridge. His eyes on the wide expanse of the sea that stretched to the end of his vision, he saw Russia that deported him as the devil and Nigeria he had been deported to as the deep blue sea.

This was the first time Morgan was on the third mainland bridge. He was surprised Nigeria has been able to build such a long bridge over the sea. The bridge stretched on and on. When he thought it was ending, it began.

'Home, sweet home,' he bellowed in a brief moment of nostalgia. 'I am home and happy. But am I?' His mind drifted to Russia.

Chapter Three

Thirty years ago, as a young man of twenty-one years, Morgan had accompanied his boss to an international conference in one of Moscow's universities. While his boss' eyes were on the conference, his eyes were on living in Russia after the conference. The light, the water, the buildings and the streets of Russia were so much better than those of Nigeria. He had also heard there were many jobs in Russia. In Russia, one worked where he wanted, left when he wanted and was paid almost what he wanted. In Russia, he would be able to make money and send home to his family relations. In Nigeria, making money to help one's relations was almost impossible because there were no jobs most of the time and most of the places. Where there were jobs, the salaries were jokes compared to Russian salaries he thought.

After the conference, Morgan's boss looked for him, but he was nowhere to be found. He had run away and was lost in the swarms of people in the streets of Moscow. Not able to find him, his boss travelled back to Nigeria alone.

For days, Morgan walked the streets of Moscow with a lot of excitement though he had little to eat. It was thrilling just walking along the streets on well laid out pedestrian walks without smelling gutters and canals. It was delightful walking the malls in a sea of white faces flanked by an array of shops displaying high quality wares of various types. It was indeed great breathing the air of Russia, walking on its soil and having its sky above his head. At some point, he would wonder if indeed he was really in Russia and not sleeping and dreaming. The Great Russia, the Heavenly Russia; how could he, the son of a poor farmer in Nigeria, be the one breathing the same air with the Russians? At such times, he would pinch himself to wake up and he would find he was not sleeping and dreaming, but truly in Russia.

He walked the streets in the day returning to sleep behind a gas station with a projected roof behind and a container that screened him from view. On the fourth day, he was employed in a restaurant as a cleaner. He was very happy. At least, he would have money to buy food. Who knows, he might even be given food by the restaurant proprietor. He was right on both scores. He was paid by the hour and given free food. For a moment, the dark cloud that hung over his life drifted away. Winter was fast approaching. With work and pay, winter would not find him outside with the bears.

He worked for the restaurant for four years as cleaner, cook and service man before getting a job as a security guard with a very good salary. As a security guard, he worked night than day shift. He was engaged by a security firm which posted him to shopping malls. When on duty, every hour he was required to go round the mall he had been posted and write a report of what he had observed during his mall-round. Before closing and going home, he was also required to write a report on the state of affairs at the time he was closing and going home.

When he took up the job of security guard, he was told he would in the course of time be promoted to supervision cadre which will take him from field operations to office work. He had worked exceedingly hard to achieve this elevation, but it never came. Though his employers seemed very happy with him, their happiness had not translated into his elevation and happiness. One day, he overheard two management staff of the security firm he was working talking about his promotion.

'I think Mr. Morgan deserves a rise,' one of the men said. 'He is about our best security guard.'

'Sure, he deserves a rise,' said the other man. 'The only problem is if you promote him and he leaves the field, who will do the job? Most of our guards you know are not as diligent as he is.'

Morgan was shocked to hear what the second man said. So, he has become the donkey that should not be relieved, he agonized. Well, he was not going to be such donkey much longer. He would find another job and leave. He found another job and left.

He was not doing badly in finding jobs, but was doing badly getting permanent residency which he had been seeking since his decision to remain in Russia. All efforts by him to get a favorable hearing from Russia's immigration office had failed. But he would not give up. He would continue to try. One day he would become a permanent resident of Russia, and thereafter a citizen.

Then he lost his job and could not find another. Without a job and money to pay rent, he was thrown out of his house by his landlord. For about a year, he was without a job and a house. He kept moving from the house of one friend to that of another like a hitchhiker on a road. During the winter of his jobless and homeless year, he came back one night from hunting for a job to the house of the friend squatting him to find the house locked with the friend nowhere to be found. The cold was so severe that night that he thought he would die before morning and indeed would have died if a passerby had not seen him and taken him to his house. On getting to the man's house, he asked to be shown the washroom where he examined his face in the mirror. He was relieved his face was still there for he thought it had been eaten up by the cold. While walking the streets, his face had been buffeted by a windchill whichever direction he faced. He was never before the wind, but always against it. He captured his ordeal in a poem:

I went out to scout for a job
The weather was a friend when I set out.
Friendly as the weather was
I wore only a Tee shirt and a hoody
And the weather hugged me in friendship.
As I walked out of home to three job shops
A friend of a weather escorted me to the shops
And I shared the long walk to the shops
Between my legs and my mouth

In conversation with my weather friend.
I had forgotten it was still зима
When the weather here is no friend.
Here at this time of the year
You can be talking with the weather as a friend
And the weather will suddenly leap for your throat
Like a famish and angry polar bear.
Yeah, I was soon called to memory
When I came out of the last job shop
The weather had turned into a chilling monster
And the road I walked
Had turned into a freezing corridor
Something of a windchill was abroad
A hungry polar bear was leaping for my throat
And I went frantic for life
As the bear went frantic for blood.
Like the palm wine tapper
Who going to Ife faces Ife
And coming from Ife still faces Ife
My face was buffeted by the windchill
Whichever direction I faced.
The wind was eating up my face.
Will I be the last meal of winter this year?
I was scared I will not make home
I was scared I will make morgue.
When I pulled the feat of making home
Against the haunt of making morgue
I found I had no home to make
I had been locked out of home
By benevolence gone malevolence
Out in a снежная буря night

I was mercifully pulled into home
By the warm hand of доброта
In the home of доброта
I presented myself to the mirror.
To see what the wind had done
I was happy my face was still there
Though as a frozen corpse.
Weather in Russia is a messenger of death.
When in a foul mood as today
It is there for anyone who wants to commit suicide
To wander into with a Tee shirt and a hoody.
It is there with a spanning morgue
Anyone who wants to commit suicide
Don't need to bother if his corpse will keep.

He spent two days in the house of his benefactor before drifting asunder to southwestern Russia where he found his most paying job as a coal miner. Working in the coal mine and doing other jobs on the side, he could feed well, send money home and even save some money. He was on his eleventh year as a miner when he was arrested by the police as an illegal immigrant and deported to Nigeria.

Chapter Four

The taxi driver dropped him at Victoria Island towards dusk. No. 27 Ahmadu Bello Way turned out to be a state liaison office. The building had seen better days before falling into the evil days it was now. Now, it was dilapidated, decrepit and ramshackle. The rain, the sun and the wind had all feasted on the building with the appetite of gluttons without the mercy of a felle - the merciful rodent. Rain had spat acid on the building. The sun had smitten it with sulfur and the wind had smeared it with a leprous hand. For years, it has been the playground and feasting hall for the sun, the wind and the rain without renovation stepping in to wipe out the footprints of the elements on the building. If it was not an eyesore, it was sure a depressing sight, especially to those who knew it during its prime.

Morgan was not sure Roland his uncle had given him the correct address. Apart from the appearance of the building which did not suggest human habitation, the building being a state liaison office could not possibly be in residential use. He again checked the address on his piece of paper and looked at the signboard before the building and found both tallying. He walked to the building and knocked. There was no response. He knocked again; this time louder.

'Yes, who is it?' a voice shouted behind the building. Though for the past thirty years Morgan had only heard this voice on phone, he immediately recognized it. It was the voice of his uncle. No one in the world had a voice like that. His uncle's voice always sounded like a small bomb going off.

'Morgan!' he shouted back full of excitement.

'Morgan?' Roland screamed as he ran out of a room behind the building. 'Morgan? Impossible'

'Yes, this is Morgan!' he said as Roland swept into his arms in a warm embrace.

'Morgan, oh Morgan,' Roland whispered holding unto him and swaying from side to side.

Morgan swayed with him. About them, the humid Lagos air flowing from the sea not far off floated to and fro.

'Morgan it has been so frightfully long,' his uncle said, releasing him from his embrace to look at his face before clasping him to his chest once more.

'Yes uncle, it has been so long,' he said. 'Life in Russia has been good and tough and one has been good and tough with it.'

'Life here has also been tough,' Roland said in a melancholic voice that contrasted sharply with his hitherto buoyant mood. He was now leading Morgan to his room behind the building. 'Where I am now living must give you an idea of how tough things have been with me of late.'

'Yeah, yeah,' he droned, his face going a shade cloudy. He was walking behind Roland as he led him to his room 'Well, uncle this is life. We take it as we find it.'

'You are right Morgan,' the uncle said, sitting down on his bed. There was only one chair in the room. He waved Morgan to it. 'I am so happy seeing you again,' he said when Morgan sat down.

'Are you now living in a state liaison office?' he asked Roland.

'As a trespasser, yes.'

'No, not as a trespasser, but as the Governor of our state,' Morgan said, laughing. 'A liaison office is like a Governor's Lodge. He who occupies it is a Governor.'

Roland laughed with him. 'I lost my job with the bank I was working,' he said. 'With no job and little savings, I could not afford to pay rent demanded by greedy Lagos landlords. Observing the liaison office not to be in much use, I talked to the man managing it and he gave me this room after I had greased his palms.'

'Wonderful,' Morgan said. 'This is Naija! A manager of a liaison office renting it out! Where else will this happen? Where is your family?'

'My wife left me when my job left me,' Roland said in a sad tone. 'She proved the vulture of fortune that does not stay a night longer than the feast. My two children are in universities in the north. During holidays, they used to come down to Lagos to hustle with me. How is Russia?' he asked.

'Uncle, Russia has rejected me,' Morgan said in tears. 'Russia has thrown me out and shut the door violently on my face.'

'What are you saying?' Roland asked in a voice full of alarm.

'Uncle, I have been deported from Russia because I have no residency papers,' Morgan said in a flush. 'Uncle I am now a deportee –высланный in Russian language. No more Russia for me.'

'This is terrible,' Roland murmured.

'Yes, it is terrible,' he muttered.

'Well, perhaps not so terrible,' Roland said with an amused expression on his face. 'You said since I am living in a state liaison office, I am something of a Governor. Now that you will be living in this liaison office with me, we can use it to liaise your way back to Russia. We can use it to liaise you into a job in our state.'

'Uncle you have not changed,' Morgan said. 'As witty as ever.'

'The tortoise never changes,' Roland said.

'Yeah,' Morgan yawned. 'My fear is that living illegally in this liaison office, we may be deported from it someday when we least expect. For me, that will be double deportation and I will not find it funny.'

'In wits, you are the true nephew of your uncle,' Roland said, laughing.

'Yeah,' Morgan muttered.

'Thinking over your deportation more seriously,' Roland said after a while of silence, 'perhaps it is not such a terrible thing. You have been in Russia for thirty years. During these years, there was hardly a month you did not send money or some other thing to one member of our family or the other. You have done very well for the family, but I don't think you have done so well for yourself. Now that you are back home and will be living with me, I will ensure you do well for yourself. You cannot continue to live only for others. You need to also live for yourself.'

'But uncle things are so tough here from what I am seeing; how can I earn a good living and do well for myself here?' Morgan said.

'No doubt, things are tough here. But other people are surviving and even prospering. We will survive and prosper with them,' Roland said.

'That's the spirit,' Morgan said with a significant improvement in his humor. 'That is the spirit.'

'Yeah,' Roland whirred, giving him a cozy look that was infectious.

'Wow! uncle,' Morgan exclaimed, beaming at his uncle. He had just recalled his discussion with the taxi driver that brought him from the airport. 'I was picked from the airport by a well-educated and informed taxi driver. 'The guy is so well educated and informed. To me, he is an elite taxi driver.'

'Yeah,' his uncle mused, looking amused. 'That's why he is running the airport patronized by the elites.'

'Uncle, you are impossible.'

Chapter Five

Morgan was closer to his uncle Roland than he was to his other relations. There was a bond between them that seemed to run deeper than the ties of kinship between an uncle and a nephew. When he was away in Russia, it was Roland his other relations kept asking about him from.

'How is Morgan,' they would ask Roland.

'He is fine,' Roland would answer without sometimes knowing if he was fine or not.

'He is fine and yet cannot send more dollars to us?' Chado an elderly man of the family queried Roland at a family meeting to discuss Morgan. Chado looked so wiry and feeble that whenever he was outside and there was a storm, his wife would yell at him to come inside lest he be blown away by the wind with litters on the ground.

Without them saying it, whenever his kinsmen asked him about Morgan Roland always knew they were not so much interested in his welfare as him sending them more money. If Morgan was washing corpses in Russia and was sending them money, not many of them would lose sleep because of this. If he had himself turned into a corpse that was sending them money, all would be jolly fine with most of them.

'They don't pick dollars on the road in Russia,' he retorted in an angry tone to Chado who asked why Morgan was not sending them more dollars if he was fine as he said.

'Then he should climb the trees they are picking them to pick them,' Tali, Morgan's aunty also at the meeting said, sullenly. She was by Roland's reckoning greedier than everyone else

'Aunty, you are saying something there,' a young man enthused.

'He is leggy and has the long hands of a palm wine tapper. He can climb any tree to pick the money,' Tali added for effect.

'If it is a matter of climbing trees to pick money, you are leggier and handy to climb all the trees in Russia and pick all the money,' Roland fired back at her. 'Why don't you get on the next plane and fly there to pick the money Morgan cannot pick?'

'Women don't climb trees,' Tali said, tartly.

'To my knowledge there is no custom or tradition against women climbing trees,' Roland retorted. 'To my knowledge, no one ordained men tree climbers.'

'Nature ordained them,' Tali rejoined. 'Women can't climb trees,' she went on petulantly.

'I see. So, when it comes to climbing trees, women are no longer the equal of men as you always assert?' Roland said with a tinge of mockery in his voice.

'I have not said so.'

'What have you said?'

Tali hissed and threw her head backward, her eyes cast wide on the open sky.

'You see Tali, although water and gin are the same color, they don't have the same taste,' his uncle said, the mockery in his voice exploding in her face.

'All these are red herrings,' Tali said, trying to steer discussion back to Morgan sending more money home. 'The issue is Morgan should be sending us more money.'

'I repeat, Morgan does not pick money on the streets of Moscow,' Roland said.

'Neither is there such place on earth where people pick money on the street,' said an elderly easy-going man not keen on discussing Morgan and money. To him, Morgan has been doing well by the family. He would rather steer the meeting to bagatelle, to trifles than censure Morgan for money. 'Talking about the palm wine tapper and palm trees always excites my interest in the palm wine tapper and his trade,' he said looking tickled.

'Always excited by palm wine tapping, I wonder why you did not take to the trade in your youth,' said Chado, peeved by the easy-going man's apparent lack of interest in getting Morgan to be sending more money.

'Chado since you love money so much, you needed to have taken to palm wine tapping in your youth than I needed to,' the easy-going man retorted. 'In fact, you needed to have also taken to rubber tapping. Both the palm wine tapper and the rubber tapper are actually tapping money from trees, not palm wine or rubber. Talking about it, I can also see the oil thief tapping money when tapping pipelines for crude oil. Perhaps you need to go out there to join the oil thieves tapping crude oil from pipelines.'

'No one is straight with anyone in this country,' someone said. 'Talking about tapping of pipelines reminds me of what I heard a young man saying to another young man some weeks ago to show how no one is straight with anyone.'

'What did the young man say to his fellow?' many voices asked together. Everyone at the meeting knew the person with the tale always had funny tales.

'He said he no longer wants to hear anyone making false promises to him that something he would be given is in the pipeline because things in the pipeline in the country never come out of the pipeline. For effect, he said which pipeline is such a person talking about with all the vandals in the Niger Delta vandalizing pipelines to tap things in the pipelines?'

Many people laughed.

There was visible pain and anger on Tali's face. Instead of the meeting focusing on Morgan sending more money than he was, trivialities were being bandied about with gusto and relish. She was boiling outside and screaming inside. Her eyes still cast on the sky were blazing disgust.

'All of you talking about tapping of pipelines are saying something of weight,' Morgan's cousin who also was not keen on discussing Morgan and money said. To him also, Morgan has been doing well by the family. 'To solve the problem of tapping pipelines by crude oil thieves, we may need to go after palm wine tappers,' he went on. 'They teach the oil tappers the tricks of their business.'

'You are also saying something there,' said another cousin who looked like he was sired by baboons which abandoned him and was adopted by humans. 'I can see something even more sinister than what you are saying. On top a palm tree, the palm wine tapper can see whoever is tapping oil anywhere, yet he would say nothing about what he saw when he climbs down the tree.'

'It is not everything the palm wine tapper sees on the palm tree that he talks about in the village,' another relation sought to remind them of a common saying.

'Whoever first came up with that saying must be a thief,' retorted yet another relation.

'You are also saying something there,' said the cousin not keen on discussing Morgan and money he should be sending. 'It might be that palm wine tappers are in league with oil thieves. They may be on top of a palm tree pretending to be tapping palm wine, when in fact they are sentinels covering the backs of oil thieves by whistling to them whenever they see anyone approaching.

'Then we have to look more closely at the activities of palm wine tappers these days,' said a relation who had not said anything since the meeting started.

'Let's pray for Morgan instead of all these talk about money,' the family head said after an interval of silence.

A prayer went out to the ancestors for Morgan to do well in the white man's land if he had not been doing well.

The meeting was in the courtyard of the head of the family. All the while the meeting had been going on, rainclouds had been gathering in the east. Though they had observed the rainclouds, they did not think rain was imminent. However, as soon as prayer was offered for Morgan, rain began to fall. The meeting was truncated by the rain as everyone ran for shelter in one room or the other.

For close to an hour, the rain went on pouring. When it was over, the meeting reconvened in the courtyard.

Chapter Six

'We talked too much about palm wine in this meeting, I believe that was why rain descended on us,' the head of the family said, jocularly when the meeting reconvened. 'Palm wine as we all know is water from the sky. Talking about it is invoking rain.

A number of people laughed.

'We have offended the god of the sky by talking too much about palm wine,' someone said.

'We need palm wine to appease the offended god,' another person said.

'How do you appease the god of the sky with water that comes from the sky?' somebody asked.

'Boja, you are saying this because, you don't know how the drunk appeases hangover,' another person said. "A mad dog has bitten me and I have gone mad!" cried a drunk in a hangover. "I am coming out of madness and I feel wretched coming out of the blissfulness of Gelung – the house of cheer. In the languor of a hangover, I want to take the hair of the dog that bit me. This is what the law of similars – the law that like cures like, is telling me."

'The point of this meeting remains why Morgan is not sending more dollars to us,' Tali said, steering the meeting back to her obsession.

'Since you don't seem to know or you are pretending not to know, they don't use dollars in Russia,' Roland said. 'They use rubbles. The dollars

Morgan has been sending to us, he purchased them the expensive way we purchase them here.'

'See what I have always suspected and said to anyone that cares to listen,' Tali said, stretching her hands wide and looking from side to side with all the drama and theatre she was capable of. 'Roland you will eventually tell the truth. For you to know the currency they are using in Russia, Morgan must have been sending not only dollars to you, but that currency as well,' she said, looking like a monkey banana has been removed from its hands. 'Because you have been eating from his palms, you won't hear anything said against him. Fine, we are watching you; at least I am.'

'You have a point there Tali. When the mad man speaks sense, you don't reject it because he is mad,' Chado said.

'Are you suggesting I am mad?'

'No, I am saying for the first time you have spoken sense,' replied Chado. 'Roland is always defending Morgan. He must have been sending more money to him than to the rest of us. He might even have been sending money to him to share with us, but he has been keeping it to himself alone. For all we don't know, money may be flowing from generous hands into stingy hands. Honey may be dripping from a honeycomb into the mouth of a honey bear.'

'Chado, don't add mudslinging to your greed; you would be too ugly to live with,' Roland said with a disdainful look on his face.

'Roland spare us your self-righteousness,' another uncle said in an acerbic tone. 'We all know how generous Morgan is.'

'Let everyone insinuate what he wants; I can't be bothered, knowing I have never appropriated to myself money meant for anyone,' Roland said struggling to keep down his rising irritation. 'We all know how kind and generous Morgan is, yet we keep saying hateful things about him,' he went on full of disgust. 'The nine lepers who walked away without showing gratitude to Jesus after he had healed them must have been reincarnated into this family. Honestly, I sometimes wonder why one was born into an ungrateful family like this.'

'Roland!' the family head bellowed in a cautioning note. Roland had moved close to spiting on the family, something he should not, however the provocation.

'I am sorry,' Roland apologized. 'It is just that some of our family members keep reminding me of Gehazi and Achan. Why are we allowing greed and ingratitude to suffocate reason and sense in us? Everyone knows it is not easy earning money anywhere in the world. This includes Russia.'

'If Morgan cannot make it big on the palm trees of Russia, he should come back home,' Boja, Morgan's cousin, said as if he had not heard what Roland said. 'Maybe he can make it big on our palm trees. A hunter does not need to go to the forest in another country to kill a lion. In fact, going to a foreign country to hunt for lions may be why the hunter would not kill lions because he does not know the forest in the foreign land and so may not know where to go in search of lions. Also, the forest there does not know him and so will not deliver lions to him. If Morgan cannot hunt well in Russia because he does not know the forest there and the forest there does not know him, he should come back home. He knows the forest here and the forest here knows him.'

'Morgan has stayed long enough in Russia for him to know the forest there and for the forest there to know him,' said another cousin. 'In fact, he had lived longer in Russia than he had lived here. So he should know the forest there than he knows the forest here and the forest there should know him more than the forest here knows him.'

'Hagui, what you are saying shows how little you know about these matters,' said Boja. 'You can never know any forest the way you know the forest you were born into. You can never be at home the way you are at home in the forest you were born into. We all hunt better in the forest our people are; in the forest we can whistle and be heard and understood. No forest can know you like your home forest because you and your home forest are one.'

'Boja, you are saying something very heavy there,' said Morgan's half-brother. 'If Morgan cannot find his way through the Russian forest, he should return home to our forest. If he cannot be useful to us in Russia, he should come back home and be useful to us.'

'You son of the Adebas that has been here with us, how much use have you been to us?' Roland flared up at the half-brother. 'All you do is scratch your buttocks shedding lice and bedbugs on everyone.'

'All these bickering and veering off to frivolities will take us nowhere,' Tali said intent on her course. 'All I know is that Morgan is making a lot of money in Russia and is eating it alone or with a few of us who are so greedy and selfish to eat it alone with him,' she said, spitefully.

'Money, money, money; how much did you contribute to send him to Russia?' Roland asked Tali exasperated to the point of screaming at her.

'How much did I contribute?' Tali muttered, looking mildly bewildered. It seemed she did not expect the question.

'You heard me.'

'Is he a prostitute?[*] Why should he be sponsored to Russia?' Tali getting her second wind hurled back at his uncle.

'From your attitude, you won't be bothered if he is gay or washing corpses in Russia so long as he sends money to you,' Roland spat back at her.

---

[*]It was common in some communities in Southern Nigeria for families to put money together to sponsor young girls to Europe for prostitution. Girls so sponsored were expected to repatriate proceeds of their prostitution home to be shared by those who invested in the scheme. Tali's response here alludes to this practice.

'How much did I contribute?' Tali murmured still smarting under the sting of the question Roland lashed her with.

'Yes, how much did you contribute? You did not invest, yet you keep screaming for prodigious returns. Only the highwaywoman behaves the way you are behaving,' Roland said with a flourish in his voice.

'Are you saying I am a highwaywoman?'

'I am not saying so. You are saying so.'

'Let's spice this meeting with some palm wine,' someone said, standing up to do a genge dance – the dance of palm wine. 'All this talk about Morgan and money is getting too serious and boring to me.'

'You heard what was said about palm wine talk. Do you want to bring another rain upon us?' someone asked.

'On the contrary I want to appease the god of the sky. Like the drunk, I am asking for the hair of the dog that bit me. I want to appease the god of palm wine that is being outraged by all this boring talk.'

For a while no one spoke.

'Did I contribute?' Tali said, breaking the silence. 'You that he has been sending money to, how much did you contribute to take him there?' she launched at Roland in a tone that sounded scornful.

'I contributed nothing, but I am getting a lot as you and everyone here is,' said Roland, sneering at Tali. 'I am not a highwayman. I still have my conscience.'

'So, I have lost mine.'

'If you had one.'

Chapter Seven

Apart from being close to Roland, Morgan decided to stay with Roland because his uncle lived in Lagos. He had been told there were more job opportunities in Lagos than elsewhere in Nigeria.

Staying with Roland in Lagos, he made several applications for employment to various public and private establishments. For one month, he scratched the streets of Lagos for a job without finding any. Tired of trekking one day, he sat down by a broken bus in Obalende motor park to rest. While he rested, he could hear motor park touts calling on passengers to board their *molue* and *danfo* buses. 'Oshodi, Oshodi, Iyanapaja!'

The din generated by the touts was distressing, but also thrilling. One of the touts in particular excited Morgan. As he blared Oshodi, his hand was on his groin as if deriving the power to shout Oshodi thence. The tout had the face that would stop a clock. Thinking he had such a face, Morgan looked at his wristwatch to see if it was working. In the politics of Nigeria, the tout was the type of person that would not fail to find favor in a contest of touts for favor.

The tout reminded Morgan of a thug his uncle told him about. At a political rally, the thug wielding knives and swords flashed the tools of his trade violently on concretes releasing sparks and flames of fire. According to his uncle, not only did the knives and swords of the thug give up sparks and flames when flashed across concretes, they scarred the concretes they were flashed. While his knives and swords ate concretes, they lost their edges when flashed on his bare throat and stomach. His knives and swords struck against each other produced flames of fire that he swallowed. A politician at the rally scouting for a political thug found in him what he was looking for. If his knives and swords could eat concretes, human flesh and bones would be pieces of cake for them. If he could swallow flames of fire, he could swallow any political violence his opponent could muster.

As the various touts competed for passengers, three passengers came into the park. They all happened to be going to Oshodi. Two touts rushed at them in a flurry. They went with the tout first to reach them. The other tout swore at the one who got the passengers. 'Your papa!' he howled.

'Your mama!' the other tout bawled back. With the new three passengers he had gotten, his bus was full and moved off with a loud screech on the eroded surface of the park. As the bus moved off, the tout who was beaten to the passengers struck its behind with a small stick he was holding.

'You hit the buttocks of your mother,' the tout in the moving bus spat at him.

The tout who was insulted laughed and went back to look for passengers for his bus.

Morgan watching and listening to all these laughed in spite of his fatigue. The touts were clearly beyond the shame and anger of insults.

To Morgan's right, a man was urinating under a tree in the full gaze of people in the park.

'Lagos *na wa*,' someone said on seeing what the man was doing.

'Lagos takes away shame,' said another person.

'Lagos takes away shame or shameless people come to Lagos,' said yet another person.

'Lagos has no shame,' the commentary drifted and floated through the park with litters that also drifted and floated through it.

'It is people that come to Lagos that have no shame. All the shameless people in the world come to Lagos. What can Lagos do?'

'I repeat Lagos has no shame.'

'I also repeat it is people that come to Lagos that have no shame.'

Morgan stretched his mind for a scenario in Russia he could compare with what he was seeing and hearing in Lagos, but could find none. In Russia life was sober, civil and peaceful on the surface. Here life was vulgar, bawdy and rude on the surface and below. As he sat perceiving activities in the motor park, he saw a man sitting on a veranda and drinking beer. The man was talking in a very lively manner and waving his hand about as if to make his point by hand as by mouth. Because of the distance between them, he could not hear what the man was saying. Tired of sitting where he was, he wandered to the man.

'I was a very young man then,' he heard the man saying when he got closer to him. 'I was full of adventure. I had no care in the world. Neither did I have caution in it. I just packed a bag and left for Germany. When I got to Germany, I could not speak German and the people I met in a bar like this also could not speak English. I wanted a job, but did not know how to tell the man I saw serving beer that I wanted a job. So, I took hold of an empty bottle, placed it on my open palm and served an empty table. The man serving the beer who happened to be the owner of the bar understood me and gave me a job that very evening. It was that easy and funny.'

Standing where he was listening to the man who was far older than him, Morgan was thrilled. If his staying back in Russia was a mad thing to do, he was not alone in his madness. If it was stupid, he was not alone in his stupidity. He drifted away from the man and headed back to Victoria Island.

As usual, his uncle was not at home when he got home. On most days, his uncle left home early in the morning and returned late in the evening. He was running a printing outfit somewhere in Obalende.

The loaf of bread he could not finish eating in the morning was still where he left it. So also the tea he could not finish. Hungry, he devoured the bread and tea and went to sit by the beach which was only a stone throw away from his home.

Sitting on the sand of the beach, his eyes wandered to a man walking towards him. Whether by practice for dramatic effect or that was how he was born, the man had a remarkably stupid expression on his face. His friends often made fond of him that if he did not accomplish anything else in life, he had achieved a feat no one else had: composing the most stupid expression a human being is capable of. Further making jest of him, they would say if there was a competition of who could put up the most stupid expression, the expression on his face was so singular and exceptional in communicating stupidity that he must win the prize.

On the shore and far into the sea, canoes were floating, some with their owners, others with no one. Before he left for Russia, he once flew to a state in the riverine areas of the country. Flying over a network of rivers and creeks dotted with canoes and small communities, he was moved to poetry:

> Canoes floating in flooded rivers
> Looked like small islands in leggy seas.
> Rivers flooded with mud and oil
> Looked like streams of mud and oil.
> Clustered habitations by the shore
> Lived on the flooded rivers in front
> And on the forest behind.
> Floating above the floating islands
> A sky flooded with clouds floated.
> Floating above the floating clouds
> He floated in a floating island in the sky.
> Through the floating clouds
> He now and then had a glimpse

Of the floats and floods beneath.

Reciting this poem in his mind which he had carried in his head since he composed it, Morgan's eyes grew misty with tears. Looking across the sea in the direction he thought Russia was, he began talking to himself: 'Dear Russia; dear homely and stately Russia, why did you throw me out in this unkindly and rude manner? I that love you so much, why did you turn me to the dogs of the streets in this uncouth and raw manner? It is so unfair. To think I will no longer step on your shores again is killing me. Red Square is gone and with it beauty; Whitestone is gone and with it life. To think I am stuck with Nigeria is doing terrible things to me.' He was crying now and the tears were flowing in torrents of bitterness and anguish. 'What did I do?' What did I do?' When he became sober, he started wondering what was happening now in a popular pub he and his Russian girl friend who later became his bitter enemy used to go to.

Chapter Eight

A year before his deportation, Morgan had gone to the pub with Alisa his Russian girlfriend. It was a popular pub they frequented and always had a whale of time when there. At the pub, they met a couple they always met. The man of the couple was Senegalese while the lady was German. They two couples got talking as they usually did.

'It is so cool out here,' the Senegalese man who went by the name Pape said.

'Yeah,' Morgan droned. 'So, cool as the other side of the pillow on a wet night.'

'*So, cool as the other side of the pillow on a wet night*,' the German girl who went by the name Edelina repeated, excitedly. 'So cute.'

'As cute as your name,' Morgan said.

His girlfriend eyed him. *As cute as your name* she thought. Was there something there? Was a secret whispering to her? Was she being told to wake up and smell the coffee? If she was, she did not like the smell of the coffee. She talked little, but thought a lot. She was no doubt more beautiful than the German lady, but men are funny. Being funny, they can hunt for a grasshopper after killing an elephant; while having a queen, they can go for a hag. Morgan was her third boyfriend that was black. Her experience with the previous two was unsavory. Yet she would not give up black guys. They excited her than white guys, though they were always besotted. No doubt, she was more beautiful than the

German girl, but with men it seemed variety trumped beauty. *As cute as your name.* It had better be only as cute as her name. If it extends to her person, that was where the trouble will be. She was a fiercely jealous person.

As soon as Morgan said what he said, he regretted saying it because he knew it will not go well with his girlfriend. He knew how sensitive she was on issues of this sort. He sneaked a look at her. The expression on her face told him what he said did not go well with her as he had feared. Her eyes had gone catty and were glittering with jealousy. Nothing told him she was upset or thinking than the color of her eyes.

'Well, you know the other side of my pillow is never cold,' he said in a disarming voice.

'Why is it never cold?'Edelina asked.

'Because Alisa here is always on it,' he said, rabidly. Again, he sneaked a look at Alisa. This time, he liked the look on her face. Her catty eyes had gone milky tender. Clearly what he said now not only went well with her, it wore well. Before he said it, he was not sure it will have this effect, but it had. He thought it had because it was a reply to Edelina and not to her boyfriend. He answered Edelina the way he had to show there was nothing between them, but there was everything between him and her. He knew how her mind worked so well.

The two couples were seated opposite each other. Edelina sitting beside her boyfriend Pape had noticed Alisa had become tense when Morgan had said what she said was as cute as her name. In both looks and intellect, she liked Morgan and won't mind going for him if he were to go for her. So when he said *as cute as your name,* the beating of her heart quickened. Was there something there? Could she hope? When she saw the jealous look on Alisa's face, she swore at her in her mind. 'Bitch, damn you,' she kept saying in her mind. 'You can't have him alone. Like champagne, he is not the sort of man one lady can keep to herself. He must go round. Thinking like this, she cast a fleeting contemptuous look at Pape. He was nowhere near Morgan in looks and brains. How did she land an asshole like him?

Neither Morgan nor his girlfriend Alisa had noticed any excitement in Edelina when Morgan had uttered his endearment. If Alisa had noticed anything near that in her, she would have been more infuriated and would have been more implacable. If Morgan had seen it, he would have been excited for he fancied her. She might not be as beautiful as Alisa, but she was more sociable and, it seemed, more caring.

Chapter Nine

Two days after their outing at the pub, Morgan was walking on a road in his neighborhood when Edelina, coming in the opposite direction, walked by.

Morgan was surprised to see her. She was not living in his neighborhood. Where did she spring from at an hour and on a day like this 'Hi!' he saluted her in a voice that carried his thoughts.

'Hi!' Edelina replied in a vivacious voice Morgan thought charming. Not only was her voice charming, the outfit she was wearing was charming. It packaged her into a moving riot of beauty.

They had both stopped walking on their sides of the road. Each seemed to be looking for an opportunity in the flow of traffic to cross the road to join the other. The opportunity first came to Edelina. She walked fast across the road. She was so fluid, alluring and graceful in her walk. To Morgan, her walk was the catty, bouncy walk of models on a fashion parade. As his friend in Nigeria would have put it, walking this way, she could make a chief priest say what the gods have not told him.

When she joined him on his side of the road, the two started talking.

'Where are you going?' Morgan asked.

'Just out for a walk,' Edelina said.

'Out for a walk in a neighborhood that is not yours?'

'Yes, out for a walk in a foreign neighbourhood.'

'Out for a walk and dressed so hot?' Morgan asked, his face alive with excitement. 'Baby, you cut a dash. Not a hair of you is out of place. You look like a million dollars. Baby, ты обаятепьна!'

Edelina giggled like a little girl on her first date. This was what she liked about Morgan: exciting expressions. 'It is good for a lady to always look hot,' she said. 'If I wasn't looking hot, you might not have seen me. If I am beautiful, you are intelligent. тыумная baby!'

'Yeah, it's good for a lady to always look hot,' Morgan said. 'The only problem is that a lady looking hot the way you are makes a guy hot; no, it melts a guy. Right now, I am melting like butter on a stove. Baby, seeing you looking this hot is doing things to me the Pope will not be happy with. What am I saying, I don't think the Pope will mind seeing you the way you are. Baby, you can be a Papacy ruination.'

Edelina was tickled pink. A wave of excitement shot through her like an electric current. Her plan was yielding the result she wanted. It was not coincidence that crossed their paths. She had planned the meeting. She knew Morgan always took a walk in his neighborhood on the road they met at the time she walked by. So she had walked by at that time hoping their paths would cross. Their paths had crossed and from the excitement she was seeing in Morgan, other things would cross.

From this day an affair sprung up between Morgan and Edelina. Within a year, Edelina was pregnant for Morgan and would hear nothing about aborting the pregnancy.

Then the shit hit the fan. Alisa found out the steaming romance between Morgan and Edelina. In Morgan's words, when the shit hit the fan, it was spluttered on the ceiling and the room was full of pong.

When the shit hit the fan, Alisa hit the ceiling, again in the words of Morgan, she hit the ceiling where the shit had been spluttered. In Morgan's words yet, neither he nor Edelina could have chosen where her fist would land on the ceiling.

Sitting with her friend Valentina who knew her affair with Morgan and how it had broken down, Alisa was sulking bad. 'The sonofabitch!' she swore, her voice thick with bile.

'Who is the sonofabitch?' Valentina asked, a little shocked by the bitterness in her friend's voice and face.

'Valentina, don't give me that; you know damn well whom I am talking about,' Alisa said with a measure of offence in her voice.

'Honestly I don't.'

'Then let's forget it.'

'Is it Morgan?'

'I told you, you know whom I am talking about.'

'Yes, I suspected he is the one, but at the same time doubted if he is the one. I doubted because a few weeks ago Morgan was the son of a queen.'

That was a few weeks ago. Now he is the sonofabitch. Fortunes change.'

'Affair has gone sour. Insults are now where compliments used to be?'

'That's how it is.

'Life!'

'As for Edelina, her nether regions are what will take her to the nether regions of the hereafter. The heaven in her waist, no the hell in her waist is what will take her to the hell of the hereafter. The dark activities in the heaven of her waist, no in the hell of her waist recommend her for the hell of the hereafter.'

'Alisa!'

'Yes.'

For Alisa, Morgan, like other black men she had dated, had failed the smell test. He was stinking like an open sewer. He had become as ugly as sin. As she could not stand his presence with her, she could not stand his presence in Russia. His stench would always reach her if he was in Russia. She went to Russian immigration authorities and reported him as an illegal immigrant. This was what led to his deportation.

When the deportation order was handed to him, he went to Alisa to tell her how unfair she was to him.

'Who told you life is fair?' she howled at him. 'As far as I can see, there is neither fairness in the design of life nor in its fabric.'

'Still, it is not fair Alisa,' he mourned.

'When you betrayed me in the whoring fields of Edelina, were you fair to me?' she spat at him. 'When you locked me out of the warm of your tender arms, leaving me to the blistering ravages of the winter of grass widowhood, was that justice?'

'Alisa ...'

'You not only deserve a kick in the ass from me, you deserve a kick in the teeth.'

'Alisa!'

'Scram, and don't leave your ass behind!' she yelled at him slamming her door in his face.

Scram and don't leave your ass behind, he repeated what Alisa had said while he sat moaning over his deportation. 'Bitch, сука, I have to give it to you that was witty if it was also as wayward as you are. *Don't leave your ass behind*! Why should it worry you if I left my ass or legs behind? Alisa you are mean. You are as mean as Teke the miser in my village. 'Fine, I have been deported. Though I did not leave my ass behind, I left my seed behind in a farm you wish were yours. Edelina you have done well for me. Though I left you behind, you were the only thing I took away from Moscow.'

From Edelina his mind flitted to rural and urban Russia, the seasons of the country, its breathtaking sights and a near fatal encounter he and his friend had when they drove out to the countryside during winter.

Chapter Ten

When Morgan had money to spare, he and his Russian friend Leonid drove to rural Russia for sight-seeing. A wolves-dragged cart on snow with a man standing or sitting on the cart and holding the reins was a sight in rural Russia he was so enamored of. A man on a galloping horse in a wilderness of snow was also a breathtaking sight to him. So also was a solitary farmhouse surrounded by snow.

One day during winter, he and Leonid drove to Zvenigorod about thirty kilometers from Moscow. A man was being drawn on a cart by wolves across a wilderness of snow. The sight was taking to Morgan who was driving. He stopped the vehicle to enjoy the sight.

'Phew! Потрясающий! This is great!' he ululated. 'The landscape, the man on the cart drawn by wolves; I don't know which sight is more heavenly.'

'This is wild Russia in all its beauty and majesty,' Leonid cooed.

'Jez!'

'When it comes to beautiful landscapes, particularly beautiful landscapes covered by snow, Russia has no match in the world,' Leonid said with pride. 'As far as landscape beauty goes on earth, Russia is a world apart.'

'With what I am seeing, I can't contest what you are saying.

'If you contest, you will lose, and lose without me rigging,' Leonid said laughing.

Morgan also laughed.

As they stood watching the man drawn by wolves, heavy snow began to fall. When Leonid saw this, he asked Morgan to turn the car round so that it faced the direction of Moscow.

'Why?' Morgan asked.

'Because if the snow is heavy as it looks like it would be, it would be difficult turning the car round to go home after the snow has finished falling.'

'Yeah, I see your point,' Morgan said, steering the car about so that it was now facing Moscow.

Before setting out, they had listened to the weather forecast. The forecast said there would be about two-centimeters snowfall which was not dangerous. The thick snow now falling would not be less than five-centimeters when it was done. Visibility was reduced to zero. There was a whiteout. The snow in the air was as opaque as the one on the ground. There was no way they could drive through this. They had to remain stationary in their car with its heater turned on.

As they sat huddled up in the car, snow in a blizzard was pouring on the car and about it. The car rocked by the blizzard was gradually being buried by the snow. It was so frightening. They were in the middle of nowhere and so could not expect much in the way of someone helping them. When they stood watching the man on a cart drawn by wolves, they did not see any human habitation. In all probability there was none. Like them, the man likely did not live anywhere near where they were. By all appearance, he was a solitary figure on a favorite sport or a man skating home in other parts on the wolves-dragged cart. If he had not gotten home, he was in all probability more in trouble than they were, with the blizzard and heavy snowfall that was looking like an avalanche.

When the car was almost completely buried, the snow stopped falling. Coming out of the car and clearing the snow on the windscreen to be able to drive was easy while the snow was still flakes of ice. It would be a daunting task if the flakes were allowed to solidify into snow around the car. Knowing this, Leonid turned on his seat to open the passenger's door as soon as it stopped snowing. Morgan also turned on his seat to open the driver's door.

Without much difficulty, they both opened their doors and cleared the snow on the windscreen. After clearing the windscreen snow, Leonid more experienced driving on snow took over the driving. Behind the wheels, he began to move the car forward.

Rural Russia was beautiful Morgan thought as they snaked through the snow towards Moscow. To him, it was more beautiful during winter than other seasons. In rural Russia, the white clouds in the sky slept on the ground in boundless wildernesses of snow during winter melting his heart with excitement. But lurking in the beauty of rural Russia during winter was death. Yes, rural Russia was beautiful during winter; but it was beautiful in a deadly way. One could step on a river or pond covered with thin ice and it would cave in drowning the person if he could not swim. The water so cold, the person could be frozen even if he could swim.

As he did not know between rural and urban Russia, which was more exciting to him, he did not know between spring and fall which he found more beautiful and exciting. During spring, everywhere was green. The whole country was turned into a huge garden exciting to his bucolic elements. During fall, the country turned orange and pink. The whole country was lighted with orange and pink lights on trees exciting to his color bias.

When the weather got it right on temperature and moisture during spring or fall, Russia was heaven on earth. On the few days the weather got it right, it was a keg of wine dripping nectar on his heart. On such days, he went into the woods. While in the woods, he leapt into the air from time to time, whooping as he did so. Then he could not imagine any earthly condition that could be more pleasurable than the one he was.

Between rural and urban Russia, Morgan could not say which was more exciting to him. When in the country, he lived in Moscow when working in Moscow and in other big cities when working in those cities or in rural areas near them. Russian cities were great cities where there was no difference between day and night. When he was not at work, he was likely to be in a pub or shopping mall. He enjoyed sitting in one place watching the world drift by. Now and then he got into conversation with a stranger. He was surprised how white people he was meeting for the first time opened up to him on matters he considered private that could only be discussed with friends or close acquaintances.

One day he was in a train sitting close to a man who turned out to be an American who had lived most of his life in Russia. The man was excited having him sit beside him. He began telling him about his wife who he said was Congolese. It was then winter. The man looking outside and seeing snow falling said his wife at home was likely to have opened all the doors and windows of their house because that was what she always did during winter, particularly when it was snowing as it was then. 'It's crazy,' he said. 'Cold doesn't get to her. It is so surprising considering she was born and brought up in Congo where there is no winter. I was born in the U.S and have lived most of my life in Russia with the worst winter in the world. Why do I feel cold and she does not?'

For a while, he could not say anything. His question was as crazy to Morgan as the behavior of his wife. He was looking for a crazy answer to meet it. 'The weather here gets crazy,' he said finally. 'I guess it makes some people crazy. The crazy weather must be making your wife crazy, man.'

'Yeah man, what you are saying sounds cool as crazy as it is,' the man said, tickled by what he had said. 'Yeah, what you said sounds hot crazy.'

He did not say anything to this. They came down at the same station. When they came down, the man followed him asking which African country he was from.'

'Nigeria,' he said.

'Nigeria? Very cool place. You are my in-law.'

'Then you have to give me palm wine or schnapps,' he said, laughing.

'What was that?' the man asked.

He explained to him that in Nigeria, a man who marries another person's daughter is required by tradition to give his father in-law palm wine – liquor produced by palm trees or schnapps which the man knew.

The man laughed heartily when he understood him. 'You are cool man. You are hot in the noggin, man,' he said when he stopped laughing.

They continued walking together and talking until they entered different buses to head to their destinations.

He had been deported from Russia and had lost all the good things of the country. 'Poor me,' he wept. 'Poor me; I have fallen through the cracks. Frost has been added to my snow and I am freezing out. It is so unfair. What did I do? How can I be deported from a country I love so much and have lived in for thirty years? Why should the disappointment and frustration of a mean woman move authority to the vehemence of deporting me? Well, at least I have a child out there. But I may never see that child. Poor me; poor child that would grow up and be asking who is my daddy?'

Chapter Eleven

Without a job in Lagos, Morgan had at least one consolation: Roland the uncle he was staying with was not making financial demands on him. He had given him accommodation and was feeding him without complaining.

When Roland lost his job with the bank, he set up a small printing business which had been struggling up to the time Morgan returned. Shortly before Morgan returned, Roland had applied for a loan from a micro-finance bank to execute a printing contract he had secured from a government agency. He was granted the loan; he successfully executed the contract and was paid. From that point, his business picked up and began flourishing. Within two months of Morgan staying with him, be bought a car and moved out of the liaison office into a rented apartment in Obalende

Tali, Morgan's aunty who lived in Maryland was angry. To her and Morgan's other relations, it was Morgan's money that had changed Roland's life. No explanation by Morgan or his uncle would make them think differently.

'How wicked and selfish people can be,' Tali mourned to Morgan when he visited her and she raised the issue again as he knew she would.

'This is where all of you got it all wrong,' Morgan said, trying to calm her down. 'I gave uncle no money. Yes, I came with some money, but uncle has never allowed me spend it on him, even on feeding myself. All the while I have been here, it is uncle that has been feeding me. The little money I came with, he advised me to open a bank account and put it there while I scout for a job. He keeps telling me I will need the money if I don't get a job fast.'

'Tell that to the baboons, and you are lucky there are so many of them in our family,' Tali hissed. 'Morgan, how can you be so selective of who to help among your relations. Fine, you have always been closer to Roland; yes, there is this bond between the two of you the rest of us do not understand; but does that make us any less your relations than him? Fine, if you will give him ten dollars, why can't you give me two?'

'I tell you aunty you are terribly mistaken,' he said. 'I have not given uncle one dollar since my return.'

'Morgan, you are not fair,' she went on as if she had not heard him. 'After all I did for you before you travelled abroad, the only way you will think of repaying me is to pack all the dollars you return home with and give Roland.'

'What did you do for me?' he asked, getting angry.

She could not immediately reply his question. It seemed she did not expect the question and so was not prepared for it. After a moment of silence, she said, 'I cannot answer that question. But your conscience should if you still have one.'

'Aunty I don't want us to quarrel over this matter,' he said in a reconciliatory tone.

'Why should we quarrel over the matter; after all I have never done anything for you,' she said in a bitter tone.

'I don't mean it that way.'

'Which way do you mean it?'

'I once returned from school hungry and you gave me food; I once borrowed money from you to pay my school fees. So you have done a lot for me,' he said.

'I see,' she said, her voice less rancorous.

'Aunty you have done a lot for me,' he continued trying to mollify her further. 'But believe me, I have not given uncle Roland any money. Uncle got a loan from a bank and executed a contract he was awarded by government. His prosperity is all his doing and nothing of mine. Why are you finding it so difficult to believe me?'

'That's your story,' Tali hissed, getting incensed again. 'The only story my mind is telling me and the only story I believe is that you came home with a lot of dollars and pounds which you gave your uncle leaving your aunty to die in penury. No problem. God is seeing the two of you and will judge the two of you.'

'All these dollars and pounds you keep talking about are not the currencies in Russia. Russia is a rubbles nation, not a dollars or pounds nation. If I need dollars and pounds in Russia, I have to buy them the way you buy them here.'

'That also is your story and Roland's,' Tali said, taking her head to one side and pushing her lips out in a hiss. 'Thirty years in Russia. Assuming you were saving only a hundred dollars, and knowing you, you will be saving three times this amount every month. Now how many months are in thirty years? Three hundred and sixty months. Three hundred and sixty months multiply by three hundred dollars. That is a lot of money. This is the money Roland wants to eat alone. We shall see.'

'You forgot I had to pay rent, feed and clothe myself; you forgot I was sending money to you when I was there. How could I have been saving so much?' he asked her.

'The pittance you were sending to us?' Tali spat. 'How could such pittance have prevented you from saving the much I believed you must have saved?'

'Aunty you call the money I sent to you all the years I was in Russia pittance? Aunty it is not fair,' he said looking very depressed.

Tali hissed.

Aunty, you are not fair to me.'

'I hear you.'

'You are allowing your imagination of what I made in Russia run wild. It is not good for your health.'

'So, you care about my health?'

'I do.'

'Then give me money.'

'Aunty.'

'Morgan,' she said, curling her lips into a snarl, 'you have been so unfair, to me in particular.'

'деньги!' he exclaimed.

'What was that?'

'деньги is money in Russian language.'

'I see,' his aunty hissed.

'OK aunty, I will give you something next time I come around,' he said, patting her on the shoulder.

'Now you are talking,' she said smiling like a monkey in a banana plantation. 'This is my nephew. I don't know the other one I have been talking to all these months.'

'Aunty!'

'My son! I know there is a lot out there.'

When she said this, he immediately regretted promising to give her some money. He was giving her the wrong signal. Well, he had promised. He had to honor his promise. A week later, he gave her twenty thousand naira. She went over the moon. 'I know there is a lot out there,' she said, affecting the delight of a witch on *walpurgis'* night. 'If only Roland is not there, all this money will be mine. Roland, God punish you,' she swore with resentment that was as sensible as visible.

When Morgan told Roland about the money he gave Tali, he was mad with him. 'Why did you do a thing like that?' he fumed. 'Why will you allow her blackmail you into giving her such amount of money?'

'Uncle I am sorry,' he said.

'Don't do it again,' his uncle admonished him, sternly.

'I will not do it again.'

'Your aunty is greedy.'

'I know.'

'When it comes to greed, the monkey trails behind her a thousand miles. Like the monkey she is, she is a shit-slinger.'

'Uncle!'

'She will take all you have if you are not careful.'

'I know.'

'She suffers from bottomless pit desires for money.'

'I know.

'You will need the money you are throwing on her.'

'I know.'

Chapter Twelve

When Morgan gave Tali the money, it was like he had opened a floodgate of demands from other relations. Apart from being greedy, his aunty was long-winded. She just couldn't keep her trap shut. Whatever her eyes saw or her ears heard, she would talk about it even if talking about it was harmful to her. When it came to talking, she often did not know where her interest was. She would just talk even if she was talking away her interest.

When Morgan gave her the money, her mouth flared open like the skirt of a ballerina in a ballet dance. She went to town with the story like the song bird that hopped from house to house singing about the coming of a new age. 'I told you people. He has money,' she said to any of her relations she met. 'How can anyone live in Russia for thirty years and return home without money? Someone like Morgan who from childhood has been a struggling person; how can he go to a country like Russia and return with his vaults empty?'

'So, it is true he is the one that has been giving uncle Roland money?' her niece whom she was talking to asked.

'I told you people from the very beginning, but you will not believe me. Which bank will give a miser like Roland money to execute a contract?'

'I wonder aunty.'

'Was it not the bank that sacked him? If it likes him that much as to give him loan, why sack him?'

'I wonder aunty.'

'Even his sack, how are we sure it was not the money of the bank that he stole that earned him the sack?'

'Ah ... aunty. Uncle Roland is not like that.'

'Shut up stupid girl; what do you know?'

'I know Uncle Roland is a miser but he is not a thief.'

'I say shut up!'

'I have shut up.'

'Which government agency in the first place will give Roland contract knowing he is too miserly to grease the palms of those who gave him the contract after he has been paid?'

'I wonder aunty.'

'Where were the contracts all the years he has been out of job and Morgan has been in Russia? Did the contracts also migrate to Russia with Morgan? The whole story is a cock and bull story concocted to pull wool over the eyes of fools. I am no fool.'

'I agree with you aunty. Morgan has money.'

'I told you.'

'Aunty, I will go to him for my school fees.'

'Your school fees? Ah ... that may be too much o ...,' Tali said, suddenly realizing that Morgan giving her niece money meant less or even no more money for her. Like the cricket which chirped all night long because it had tene nuts in its hole only in the morning to find all the tene nuts had been stolen by worms while it sang, she had sung herself into an empty hole. Looking at her niece, she actually looked like a worm. She was incensed to malevolence.

'But aunty, you said he is loaded with money,' she heard her niece saying.

'Ye-s I said so,' she stammered. 'But when I said so, I wasn't that sure. Remember I am not living in his bank account.'

'I see,' her niece said in a languorous tone.

'I am not saying you shouldn't try your luck,' she said, trying to dispel any suspicion her niece may have of her motive.

'I will surely try my luck,' her niece said.

Whoever Tali met among Morgan's other relations, her conversation with such person was not substantially different from that between her and her niece: Morgan had money and wads of it. It was Morgan that was funding Roland. All the talk about contracts is crap from mouth to air.

Morgan was inundated with demands from all sides. Having given some money to his aunty, he had to give to his other relations, however little.

Chapter Thirteen

Six hundred kilometers away from Lagos, the Kusha family was meeting. The return of Morgan their kinsman has filtered to them in the sleeping village of Baito. Among other things, they were meeting to discuss the return of their kinsman.

'We heard that our son Morgan has returned from the white man's land,' the head of the family and chairman of the meeting said, opening discussion on Morgan.

'So, we also heard,' an elder at the meeting said.

'But why has he not come home to tell us he has returned?' the family head said more in wonder than question. 'We prayed for him when he was there.'

'You are talking of praying for him when he was there; we gave birth to him and brought him up to go there,' an elder said.

'The ways of the new generation are strange to us the old ones,' another elder said. 'How can someone who has been away from his father's land for more than thirty years not think of coming to his village on return from his sojourn in a foreign country? If for nothing, to see his father's and mother's graves. This attitude is as foreign to me as the foreign land he travelled to.'

'His attitude of not coming home is the strange attitude of the alien land he travelled to,' someone said.

'I pray to remain a stranger to this kind of attitude,' said another person.

'Does he think we want his money?' somebody wondered.

'Those who want his money are in Lagos with him,' Chado said. 'That is why they are not at this meeting. They are in Lagos with him chopping his money. No one here needs his money. We only want to see his face which is becoming blurred in our minds.'

'We are talking about money; I heard Morgan returned without money and even without good clothes,' Boja, said. 'They said the white man does not allow anyone to leave his land with money he made there. Whatever money you make in his land, he takes away through taxes and phony bills. The white man is like the world: You bring nothing to him; you take nothing out of him. As you came, so shall you return, and that is empty handed.'

'Boja, you can't be serious,' Chado said, an expression of alarm mixed with fear overrunning his face. He had hoped if Morgan comes home, he would give him money to treat his arthritis.

'I am very serious,' Boja said. 'Morgan while in Russia could not send us a lot of money because all the money he was making was swallowed by taxes and phony bills. In the white man's land, you have to pay insurance on your car every month and pay for parking your car in front of the house you are living in whether the house is your own or you are renting it. If the house belongs to you, you also have to pay monthly for the ground it was built. That is what the white man calls ground rent. If you are renting the house, ground rent would be included in your monthly rent. So you also have to pay ground rent. All the while we were here flaying Morgan for not sending us money, he was being skinned by taxes and bills in the white man's land.'

'Boja, you can't be serious,' someone said.

'I wish I weren't.'

'I have also heard the only thing Morgan returned home with is speaking through the nose like the white man,' a middle-aged man at the meeting said, trying hard to restrain himself from laughing. Though he did not laugh, a few people at the meeting did.

'Konde, what you heard is what I also heard,' said another man, sitting behind the head of the family. 'I heard that Morgan lost everything in Russia, including his tongue. The only thing he returned home with is his nose.'

Many people laughed at this.

'Poor Morgan,' someone said while the people were still laughing. 'Without a long nose, he is speaking through his stub nose leaving his thick lips without work. The white man has a long nose and thin lips. So, his beaky nose helps his thin lips to speak.'

'Morgan went to fish in the white man's river and returned even without his fishing net,' a well-educated member of the family who had not spoken since the meeting started said. 'We go to fish in their rivers and return empty handed. They come to fish in our rivers and go home with their boats filled with fish. They send goods here which we buy at exorbitant prices and they take the money home; we send our young girls to them to prostitute and they bring back HIV to us. They set up industries here which breed pollution for our environment, bleed labor from our young men and money from our pockets; the only industries we have in their land are our young girls prostituting for farthings and our young men laboring for chicken feeds.'

'If all of you saying these things knew all you are telling us now, why didn't you tell us before so that we don't lash at him the way we were?' the head of the family said trying to refocus the talk on Morgan.

'I only got to know my own part of the tale on his return,' Boja said. 'About a week ago, I ran into a friend of Morgan living in Lagos. He was the one that told me what I said here.'

'If what all you people are saying is true, why did Morgan stay this long in the white man's land?' an elder asked. 'Why did he not run away? Was he under detention?'

'That is one of the strange ways of the new generation,' another elder said, taking a sweeping look at where most of the young men of the family were sitting. 'While in the olden days people run away from slavery, today people struggle to be slaves. For food and the wears of modern life, virgins even beg to be raped by those who can give them food and wears of refinement. Electricity, pump water, good roads, beautiful cars, skyscrapers, fast food, fine clothes, are some of the exotic things that excite our youths into slavery.'

'You forgot to mention other things,' Boja interjected.

'What did I not mention?'

'Prospects of good jobs, good healthcare, good education for children, civil and orderly life in society.'

'Yeah, those as well,' someone said, waving his hand in a dismissive manner. 'All these things Boja and Anko enumerated are what make for high standard of living. Of course, high standard of living means high cost of living which many black people in the white man's land can't afford. Though they can't afford these things, they hung on in the vain hope that they can.'

'Some of them know they can never afford these things, but they hung on so that they can continuously see these things or smell them,' Boja said, his voice reeking with scorn.

'Black man don suffer,' someone said, rhetorically.

'And he can't blame anyone for his suffering,' another person said. 'If he was not so selfish, greedy and corrupt, he would have provided for himself and his people the things he and his people are rushing to the white man's land for. He is the chief architect of his misery.'

'If the white man was as stupid, greedy and corrupt as the black man, he won't provide for himself and his people the high standard of living the black man and his people are rushing for in his land.'

'It is sad.'

'It is indeed sad.'

'Because our people are cursed with stupidity which leads them to corruption, we can't afford high standard of living,' Boja said.

'Boja, you have said something there,' someone said. 'Corruption is against intelligence.'

'Corruption is stupidity.'

'Intelligence will tell you that the welfare and wellbeing of everyone is your welfare and wellbeing.'

'Corruption has set African nations ablaze with misery.'

'And so our people keep fleeing abroad for mirages and illusions.'

'It is sad.'

'It is indeed sad.'

'As I heard, even now that Morgan returned, he did not do so of his own volition. He was deported, Boja said.

'Deported?' many voices asked in unison.

'Yes, deported. 'He is now over fifty years. His strength has started failing him. He can no longer do their *boyi-boyi* work the way he used to. So, he is deported back to us when he can also not climb the palm tree here with the agility he used to in his youth.'

'This is unfair.'

'Why grieve over what you already know?' someone said. 'There is no fairness in the world, Because there is no fairness in the world, you have to be fair to yourself.'

'Where is Tali?' someone asked, rather rhetorically.

'Tali is not here,' Boja answered. 'Tali is weeping in Lagos. She has found out that Morgan did not return with boxes of money.'

Two or three people laughed at what Boja had said.

'Someone should go to my house and bring palm wine,' an elder at the meeting said. 'We need palm wine to be able to laugh at the situation we find ourselves.'

Two young men ran out of the house of the family head to bring the palm wine. They were soon back with a big jerry-can of palm wine.

'To our ancestors,' the head of the family said pouring the first cup of palm wine from the jerry-can on the ground. Before they could drink, the ancestors must drink. Before the ancestors could hear their prayers, their thirst must be quenched.

'Our land is sick with stupid thoughts ...,' the head of the family began his supplication. 'Our ancestors heal our land ...'

'Tete, Awuu,' the meeting chorused.

'You live in the soil. Make our crops grow ...'

'Tete, Awuu.'

'You live in the sky. Make rain fall on our farms ...'

'Tete, Awuu.'

'Give us wisdom so that we go through life with less broken pots ...'

'Tete, Awuu.'

'Our kinsman who just returned from the white man's land, give him sense to come back home to his people.'

'Tete, Awuu.'

Chapter Fourteen

It seemed the ancestors did not answer the prayer of Morgan's people for him to go home to them; for instead of Morgan thinking of going to his village, he was intent on remaining in Lagos. Several times Roland had asked him to go home and greet his other uncles, but he had refused.

'Uncle, since my father's and mother's death, you are the only person in our family I can truly call my own,' he said when Roland stepped up pressure on him to go home.

'That is not true,' Roland said. 'Beside me, you have other relations. Yes, I know some of them don't care much about you or indeed anyone beside themselves, but we have to continue to care about them.'

'You know uncle, I always care,' Morgan said in a drawl. 'But the shame of failure is too much uncle. I can't go home in my current condition. May be later when things improve.'

'Which failure are you talking about, Morgan? You have not failed.'

'Uncle, I have failed.'

'I said you have not failed.'

'Uncle, I have failed.'

'Well, I have said my own,' his uncle said in a solemn tone. 'Let no one in the village accuse me of monopolizing you.'

'Why should anyone accuse you of monopolizing me?' Morgan asked. 'Am I treasure to be monopolized?'

'Now that you have returned from the white man's land, you are a lot of treasure to our people,' his uncle said. 'Most of them think you returned with a ship of money and I am the one enjoying it with you. For example, your aunty Tali thinks so.'

'You see what I am saying? You see why I don't want to go home in my current condition?' Morgan said in a depressed tone. 'I only returned home with shame, and I don't think many of them will like sharing it with me.'

'Well, you have to first make the offer and see if they will smile at you,' his uncle said, chuckling. 'You never can say.'

'If my experience with aunty Tali is anything to go by and I think it is, I know what to expect and that is why I am sparing myself the agony of making the offer,' Morgan said without a rise in his humor. 'In this life, very few people like sharing shame with you. The only thing people like sharing with you is wealth and honor, and I have very little of these now. I so much like you uncle because unlike others, you don't mind sharing my dishonor and shame with me.'

'You are my nephew. Why should I not help you carry your cross some of the way. Even Simon who was no relation of Jesus helped him carry his cross some of the way,' Roland said, patting him on the back.

'You are not the only uncle I have. I have other uncles. How many are as kind-hearted as you are?' Morgan said in a voice bleeding emotions.

'How market?' Roland asked changing the topic.

'I don't get it,' Morgan said, looking puzzled.

'I know you won't get it,' Roland said, laughing. 'You have been away for so long that some of our expressions would be lost to you; that is if you knew them before you left. '*How market*? is an Igbo trader's inquiry of how business is going?'

'Interesting,' Morgan said with a visible improvement in his cheer.

'Yeah, interesting,' Roland said. 'In fact, they have extended the expression to politics. *How market* in politics is an inquiry to a politician or a political hanger-on whether he is being patronized with the bonanza and largesse of office.'

'Our language is always not far from corruption,' Morgan said in a sad tone. 'In fact, our language is always embedded with corruption.'

'You can say that again,' Roland said with verve.

'*How market*?' Morgan crooned without improvement in his cheer. 'In my case, I am neither in business nor politics. If you say *How market to me,* what are you asking me?'

'I am asking you, how is the struggle for job and survival?' Roland said. 'There is no corruption embedded in this one.'

'Yeah,' Morgan grunted.

'A sister expression to *How market* in the Igbo man's trading lexicon is *We don sell market*?'

'We don sell market?' Morgan repeated what his uncle said. 'How can you sell market? Is market an article of trade to be sold? I thought market is the place articles are to be sold and purchased, not itself sold and purchased?'

'You are right in your thinking. The Igbo trader also thinks like you, but because of poor education expresses his thinking imperfectly,' Roland said full of mirth. He had just remembered a funny story he picked on the road related to *We don sell market*?

'Uncle you look like you want to laugh; what is it?' Morgan asked infected by the glee on his uncle's face.

'I just remembered a funny story about *We don sell market*? Roland said the mirth on his face expanding.

'What is the story?' Morgan asked. Whatever story is making Roland this jolly must be funny indeed.

'An Igbo man was lying critically ill in hospital. His sale boy went to visit him to see how he was getting on. As soon as the boy came to stand by his bed in the hospital, before the boy could ask him how he was getting on, the sick man who could barely lift his head from the pillow was asking the boy, 'Chinedu, we don sell market?'

Morgan laughed. Roland laughed with him.

Chapter Fifteen

Though Morgan was staying with Roland, it took Roland four months to ask him his experience in Russia in more comprehensive details. He could see Morgan was really traumatized by the experience and wanted to give him healing time before raising an issue his nephew would surely find pricking, if not irksome. When by his gauging, he felt Morgan had substantially put behind him his tough experience in Russia, he broached the issue with him one evening when they were both at home.

'It was rough uncle,' he said with a gloomy expression on his face. 'Often I worked three jobs to be able to pay my bills and send some money home.'

'Doing three jobs?' Roland asked, shocked.

'Yes, three jobs uncle,' he said, rapidly. 'Working three jobs often means working eighteen hours.'

'Working eighteen hours? What time then do you have to sleep?' Roland asked, alarmed.

'Sometimes four hours; sometimes only three or even two.'

'What!'

'That was how it was uncle,' he said dejectedly. 'Sometimes because of fatigue, I would be working and sleeping, and doing so in a factory can be extremely dangerous. You can walk into a machine that will chop off your head or hands. Sometimes, I would be so tired that my legs and hands would feel as if they would fall off. Sometimes my legs and hands would even feel as if they are not part of my body. Tired, I sometimes oversleep and go late to work where I would be queried or sacked for black time. If sacked, I had to go on a job hunt to be able to pay my bills and send some money home.'

'Queried or sacked for black time, what does black time mean?'

'It means tendency of blacks to be late,' Morgan said.' As he spoke, he had observed tears shining in Roland's eyes as he sat listening to his hard time in Russia.

'During winter, the ordeal gets worse,' Morgan continued in the same woeful tone. 'When I had no car, I sometimes trek to work or from work under biting cold. There was a night during winter that I came back from hunting for a job to find a friend I was squatting with had locked me out. That night I would have died of cold if a kind soul had not taken me into his house. There was also a day I suffered frost bite. It was the most painful experience I had ever gone through in my life. It was winter. I went out without hand gloves. When I returned home, my fingers were frozen. Not knowing the consequences, I stretched my frozen hands over the electric cooker to warm them. The searing pain that went through me is the most severe pain I have ever gone through. I wept like a little child.'

The tears in Roland's eyes were still welling and about to flow. Though Morgan's uncle, he was only five years older than Morgan. Right from their childhood, he had always liked Morgan and it was clear Morgan had always liked him. One of the reasons he had always liked Morgan was Morgan's love for their family and spirit of sacrifice. Morgan could easily forfeit his right if doing so would benefit a member of the family. Such spirit was rare. As they grew up, he could see the altruistic spirit in his nephew becoming more and more entrenched. This made him love Morgan the more.

'You went through all these just to be able to pay bills and send money to us?' Roland asked Morgan after a thoughtful silence.

'Yes, uncle.'

'And yet you talk of failure and shame?' Roland could no longer stop the tears from falling. For quite a while tears that had been welling in his eyes kept flowing down his cheeks. The sight of his weeping uncle also moved Morgan to tears. For a while both uncle and nephew sat saying nothing while silent tears flowed on their cheeks.

'You went through all these and couldn't tell me anything of what you were going through in any of our telephone conversations?' Roland said when he had calmed down sufficiently to speak.

'I am a man,' Morgan said. 'As a man I had to fend for myself and my family. That is what every responsible man should do.'

'Oh no Morgan, talk no more of failure and shame. You have succeeded more than anyone in the Kusha family,' Roland said in a declarative tone.

'Uncle, you are the only one in our family that thinks I am a success in my current condition,' Morgan said in a despondent tone. 'As far as other members of our family including myself are concerned, I am a failure.'

'Cold ate you, the wind clawed you for our sake and all some ungrateful members of our family can do is to keep maligning you and asking you for more money,' Roland went on as if he had not heard what Morgan said. 'It is unfair.'

'That is life uncle,' Morgan said. 'Life is rarely fair.'

'Yeah, that is true,' Roland said. 'But if life is not fair, we should at least be fair to our own. Morgan, you are our own.'

'One of the jobs I did was coal mining,' Morgan continued his story. 'While working the mines, I was constantly under the fear the mine would collapse on me and fellow miners burying us alive. At the beginning of my working in the mines, I did not know I suffer the fear of collapsing mines in common with other miners. But later, I got to know that not only miners in the mines I worked suffer this fear, but miners everywhere in the world. For instance, because of this fear, silver miners in Potosi in Bolivia worshipped the devil who they called *Eltiyo*. They believed it is the devil that makes a mine to collapse on miners. So they worshipped the devil so that he would spare them the evil of collapsing mines.'

'This is interesting,' Roland said alive with enthusiasm. 'Why should they believe the devil causes a mine to collapse?' he asked.

'The tunnel and dark conditions of a mine cannot but remind one of hell,' Morgan said. 'Reminded of hell, the devil comes to mind; the devil coming to mind, belief in what the devil can do also springs up.'

'I see,' Roland murmured in a thoughtful tone.

'The approach of the miners of Potosi may not make moral sense, but makes practical sense,' Morgan went on. 'God does no harm. It is the devil that does harm. Rather than worship God to protect them from the devil, they worshipped the devil directly. Usually they made sacrifices of a sheep or chicken to *Eltiyo*. Among the miners of Potosi, you either spilled the blood of a goat, sheep or chicken for *Eltiyo* or the next blood to be spilled could be yours.'

'This is quite interesting,' Roland said, marveling at what Morgan just said.

'Yeah, it is interesting,' Morgan rejoined.

'What were miners in your own mines doing to secure themselves?' Roland asked after a moment of silence.

'Unlike miners of Potosi, we prayed to God and hoped no mine collapses on us,' Morgan said.

'I wish you were also making sacrifices to the devil like the miners of Potosi; not only sacrifices of sheep or chicken, but of human beings,' Roland said in a mirthful tone that contrasted sharply with his hitherto mournful tone.

'Why are you saying so?' Morgan asked surprised by what his uncle said and the cheerful look on his face.

'You would have sacrificed Tali or any of the other eight lepers of our family,' Roland said, breaking into laughter. 'I wouldn't mind you sacrificing any of them if that would secure your life. You have always sacrificed for the family. It wouldn't have been a bad idea to sacrifice some of our greedy and ungrateful family members for a change.'

'Uncle!' Morgan droned.

'Are you surprised?'

'I am.'

'It means you don't know your uncle very well.'

'Hmm ...'

'What of your deportation? What really happened?' Roland asked. Having waited this long to ask Morgan about his experience in Russia, he wanted them to talk about everything so that he needed not bother his nephew again on the matter.

'Well, uncle it was all about woman palaver,' Morgan said with a melting heart. Omitting little, he went on to tell his uncle his entanglement with Alisa and Edelina which led to his deportation.

'You did bad here,' Roland said in a rebuking tone.

'I know.'

'You don't go out with the friend of your girlfriend.'

'I know.'

'Our custom forbids it.'

'I know.'

'You are not a water snake to eat on both sides of the river.'

'True uncle.'

'Yet, there is a good thing in the bad thing you did,' Roland said, his stern face going genial. 'You have a child in Russia. How do we bring him or her home?'

'That is the problem uncle and it is a hell of a problem.'

Chapter Sixteen

Nine months after Morgan's arrival in Nigeria, his uncle Roland died. What killed his uncle, he did not know. He was a healthy and active person to the point of his death. Morgan had returned from Ikeja where he had gone to submit an application for a job to find Roland clutching his stomach and writhing on the floor in severe pains. He was sweating profusely and was apparently in the throes of death. By his side was the plate of rice and beans he was eating before he was seized by the pains he was under.

Though in severe pains, Roland saw and recognized him before he died. He could see the recognition in his eyes. He opened his mouth to speak to him, but all that came out of his mouth was Ta ... Ta ... then he closed his mouth in death. It was so awful.

Morgan was distraught. Roland had taken care of him since his return to Nigeria. Even before his uncle's finances improved, he had never asked him for a dime. Among his relations, Roland was a freak of nature. While all his other relations were only interested in the dollars and pounds he returned home with, Roland was only interested in helping rehabilitate and giving him a new start in life.

With Roland dead, he had to slog it out on his own. Well, some of the money he came back with was still in his bank account. Roland had always told him he would need it. Now he needed it. No doubt, it has been depleted by demands of his relations, but he still had in the account something to live on at least for a while.

After Roland died, Tali asked him to move in with her. Without giving the matter much thought, he agreed and moved to her place. Before travelling to Russia, he has been someone who liked living with his relations. When he returned, he found his fondness of living with relations still very strong. However, despite his fondness for family cohabitation, after moving to stay with Tali, he started wondering if it was a smart thing to do. Was it not wiser to rent a small apartment somewhere in Oshodi or some other low cost neighbourhood and stay alone than with his greedy aunty? Will living with her not mean giving her money all the way?

He was right in his fears. Every day since he began living in Tali's apartment, it was one financial demand after the other. Breakfast always came from him, so also lunch and dinner. For three months at a stretch, he was the one feeding her entire family of six children and herself. She was working with the local government and had a hair dressing saloon which was doing very well before Morgan went to stay with her. When he started living with her, it was like she was no longer paid a salary and the saloon had packed up. The person she called her husband was not living with her and by all showing was not giving her much. Later, Morgan was told he was living with his mistress somewhere in Okokomaiko and it was the mistress that was taking his money.

When Morgan complained of her incessant money demands, she said she was no longer asking him to give her free money, but to lend her. Several times he lent her money, but she did not repay any. One day when he sat down thinking of her lack of shame in asking him to give her money, the exchange at Obalende Motor Park more than a year ago came to him:

Lagos has no shame.
It is people who come to Lagos that   have   no
shame.
What can Lagos do if shameless people choose to
come to Lagos?

Whichever line of this exchange was true, it was true of Tali. If Lagos had no shame, she was shameless Lagos walking the streets of Iko. If it was people that came to Lagos that had no shame, she was the matron of the shameless people that came to Lagos.

Because Lagos has no shame or because she was a shameless person that came to Lagos, Tali continued to ask him of money. When he could no longer give because he had nothing to give, she threw him out of her home; in his words, she also *deported* him out of her house because he had no papers – money, to give her.

On the streets, he went to the church he was attending to seek accommodation where he could stay for a while. The church took him in. He wanted to undertake a theological course that would make him a pastor, but had no funds to do so; neither was the church ready to sponsor him. When the church grew tired of him, it also *deported* him unto the streets.

For days, he roamed the streets of Lagos with his few belongings in his tattered bag with nowhere to stay. At night, he found a shack to sleep. He thought of going back to his village, but shame would not let him. Since Lagos has no shame, this was where he should live out the shame of his life.

One night while sitting by a roadside boulder grieving his uncle's death, a thought that had been festering in his mind since his uncle died became more poignant and pressing. Ta ... Ta ... What was his uncle trying to tell him? Was he trying to tell him something about Tali his aunty? What killed his uncle? Was he poisoned? Who poisoned him? Oh no, his aunty couldn't have poisoned his uncle; what for? His money? Oh no! He had no money worth killing anyone for. But did his aunty know this? Oh no ... Money! Why has деньги acquired such force in the native mind? деньги is pronounced as den'gi which sounds like *dangi* in Hausa language. *Dangi* in Hausa language means clan. Why then is den'gi tearing clans apart instead of forging them?

After a week of roaming the streets without a home, Segun a man known in Mushin as a kindhearted man gave him his garage to stay for as long as he wished. He stayed there for seven months. During those seven months, there was nothing Morgan and Segun did not discuss.

'Lagos has no shame,' Morgan always said to Segun. 'It is in Lagos I intend to live out my shame because people in Lagos will not see it.'

'Morgan, go back home,' Segun would tell him. 'There is not much for you in Lagos.'

'No, Segun, there is a lot for me in Lagos,' Morgan would say. 'My life is shameful and there is no shame in Lagos. Lagos is where I will live out my shame without anyone seeing it.'

'Morgan, go back home.'

'Segun, I am going nowhere. I am a высланный – a deportee from Russia with nothing to show back home. Even my aunty and the church had deported me from their quarters. It is better for me to live out my shame here where there is no shame.'

Because of the frequency Morgan called himself a deportee, Segun later took to calling him the deportee. After seven months of living in Segun's garage, Morgan disappeared leaving his belongings in the garage with no trace or message of his whereabouts.

Chapter Seventeen

Along a sleeping street in Ebute Meta, a tall, gaunt man with slouched shoulders moved, sometimes with sweeping strides, sometimes with slow, halting steps. Slightly stooping, the man on the solitary road appeared to be carrying the weight of the world on his head though he was neither carrying anything on his head nor in his hands. He was not dressed in rags, but was not dressed in fine garments either. Shirt brown, trousers milky hair tousled and tangled, the shrunken man picking the street like a chameleon was Morgan the deportee.

Walking along the backwater street, Morgan sometimes bent down as if to pick something from the ground, sometimes as if to remove something from his footwear. From his appearance, he had not had a bath for months. As he walked the street, his mouth was mumbling something no one could hear. Down the road, his mumblings turned to audible words. 'I am Morgan the deportee. The deportee from Russia. I had a good case. Why did they not see the goodness in my case? Alisa had no case. Why did they see any case in what she told them? What is the world turning to seeing cases where there are none and not seeing cases where there are?

'Papers. They said I had no papers. What nonsense, what rubbish papers did I not have? I wasn't born with papers? Which papers are they talking about? Papers; what is the use of papers in the world? God punish papers. God punish those who make papers. God punish who asked me to show him papers. Papers; where are they? Why should papers be valued more than human beings? Screw papers! Drown papers!

'But why did I not return to Nigeria after that conference? Why did I run into Moscow? Why did I so much fancy the Third Rome? What was I looking for in the First Throne? The lights? The streets? The water? The jobs? Oh my God! Where am I? Whose child, am I? Why is life so hard and mean to me? My poor child in Moscow, are you there? Edelina, where are you? Where is our child? Has that bitch Alisa come after you? Has she gotten you deported to Germany? Shall we ever see again? Shall we ever see again? My life has become too heavy for me to carry. Who will help me carry my life? Who will help me?

'Oh no, everyone is also labouring under the weight of his own life. There is no one to help me. Everyone is heaving and panting under the weight of his own life. Everyone is out of breath from the labor of carrying his own life.

'The harvest of my life is a poor harvest. It is not like the bounty harvest in my father's farm. I went as far as Russia to farm when my father could haul in so much harvest by farming only in our backyard. What seeds did I plant in my farm to have this poor harvest or did I not plant any seed? Why am I reaping a whirlwind when I haven't sown the wind? There is no head or legs in what I am seeing before me.'

For a while, he lapsed into silence. After walking a couple of paces in silence, he stopped walking and cast his gaze wide. There was nothing ahead of him on which his gaze could be said to be on. It was a blank, unbounded gaze. Then he began walking and talking again. 'If no one needs me, I need no one. But is it human to need no one? No, I need everyone and I think everyone needs me.

'Moscow how are you today? How are the lights of your streets? Where are the streets themselves? How are your waters? How are your shopping malls? Who is eating what in your pubs? Who is drinking what in your bars? Where is snow falling? Why is everywhere so quiet and unhappy here? Has the world died here?

'I am a lie, Russia is a lie, Moscow is a lie, Alisa is a lie. Only Edelina and our child are the truth. Alisa, you must have me? Says who? Was I born for you? Did I go to Russia because of you? Damn you Alisa, damn you. Alisa go to hell! Yes, go and rot in hell. But there is no hell. Hell and the devil died long ago. That is why all the evil people I see in the world are still hanging around. If hell and the devil were still alive, they would have long swallowed all the mess I see around me.

'The coal-miner has been thrown out. *Shakhtor* has been shown the door the whitish way. Help! I have fallen through the cracks and gone to seed. I am lost in the confusion of my life and can't find myself. But who is not lost in the confusion of his own life? It is all so dark and hopeless.

'My uncle Roland; my dear uncle, where are you? They said you died. Why did you die? Why should someone with your heart of gold die leaving aunty Tali with a heart of thistles? Why is life so sick, rotten and unfair? Why?'

Segun driving along the street Morgan was saw the gangling figure of the deportee but did not immediately know it was Morgan. But as he drew nearer the figure, and on a closer look, behold it was Morgan the deportee.

'The deportee!' Segun hollered, stopping his car and coming out.

There was nothing to show Morgan heard him as the gangly figure of the deportee drifted away from him. 'Morgan!' he hollered again. Again, Morgan showed no sign of hearing him.

'Morgan!' he called a third time.

This time, Morgan turned and looked at him and laughed. 'Edelina are you the one calling me? Edelina, where are you? Where is our baby?' Where is our baby, Edelina?'

Tears shone in Segun's eyes as he watched the gawky figure of Morgan floating away from him. 'Life,' he murmured in deep sorrow. 'In addition to the shamelessness of Lagos, it seemed the deportee needed madness to cope with his shame. 'Life!'

A Glossary of Russian Words and Phrases

деньги – Money. деньги is pronounced den'gi

доброта – Kindness. Доброта is pronounced dobrota.

высланный – Deportee. Высланный is pronounced vyslannyy.

снежная буря – blizzard. снежная буря is pronounced metel.

сука – bitch. сука is pronounced suka.

Потрясающий – Terrific. Потрясающий is pronounced potryasayushchiy.

Shakhtor – a derogatory Russian word for a coal miner that depicts him looking as dark as the coal he mines. The term is used derogatorily on blacks.

ты обаятепьна – you are intelligent. ты обаятепьна is pronounced ty umnyy.

ты умная – you are beautiful. ты умная is pronounced vyprekrasny.

зима – winter. зима is pronounced zima.